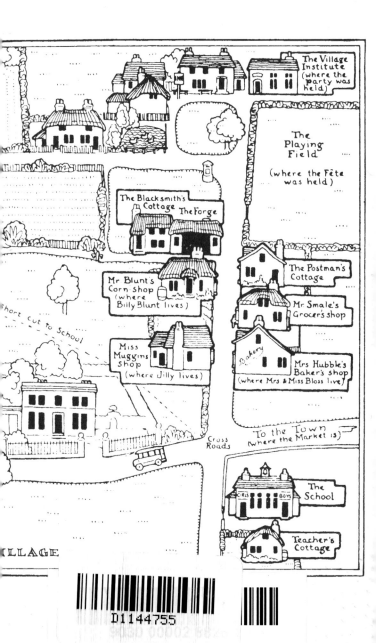

The Village Institute (where the party was held)

The Playing Field

(where the Fête was held)

The Blacksmith's Cottage The Forge

The Postman's Cottage

Mr Blunt's Corn-shop (where Billy Blunt lives)

Mr Smale's Grocer's shop

Short cut to School

Miss Muggins shop (where Jilly lives)

Bakery

Mrs Hubbke's Baker's shop (where Mrs & Miss Bloss live)

To the Town (where the Market is)

Cross Roads

The School

GIRLS   BOYS

Teacher's Cottage

...ILLAGE

MILLY-MOLLY-MANDY'S

Spring

Milly-Molly-Mandy books

Adventures
Family
Friends
School Days

Spring
Summer
Autumn
Winter

Joyce Lankester Brisley

MILLY-MOLLY-MANDY'S Spring

MACMILLAN CHILDREN'S BOOKS

The stories in this collection first appeared in
Milly-Molly-Mandy Stories (1928)
More of Milly-Molly-Mandy (1929)
Further Doings of Milly-Molly-Mandy (1932)
Milly-Molly-Mandy Again (1948)
Milly-Molly-Mandy & Co. (1955)
Published by George G. Harrap & Co. Ltd

This edition published 2012 by Macmillan Children's Books
a division of Macmillan Publishers Limited
20 New Wharf Road, London N1 9RR
Basingstoke and Oxford
Associated companies throughout the world
www.panmacmillan.com

ISBN 978-1-4472-0804-4

1 3 5 7 9 8 6 4 2

A CIP catalogue record for this book is available from the British Library.

Printed and bound in China

Publisher's Note
*The stories in this collection are reproduced in the form in which they appeared
upon first publication in the UK by George G. Harrap & Co. Ltd.
All spellings remain consistent with these original editions.*

Contents

The Nice White Cottage with the Thatched Roof (where Milly-Molly-Mandy lives)

The Meadow (where M·M·M and Billy Blunt practised racing)

The Barn (where M·M·M gave a party)

Brook

The Moggs's Cottage (where little-friend-Susan lives)

Short cut to School (only used in dry weather)

Woods

To Another Village

MAP of the

Joseph Bradley

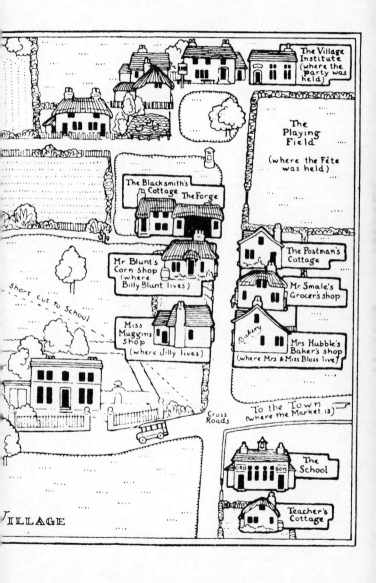

Milly-Molly-Mandy Goes Motoring

Once upon a time Milly-Molly-Mandy had a lovely invitation.

The little girl Jessamine, who lived in the Big House with the iron railings by the cross-roads, came round to the nice white cottage with the thatched roof one Saturday morning to see Milly-Molly-Mandy.

She walked up the path and knocked at the door, and when Milly-Molly-Mandy (who had seen her through the window) ran to open it the little girl Jessamine said, "Hullo, Milly-Molly-Mandy! Mother and

I are going in the car to have a picnic on the Downs this afternoon, and Mother says would you like to come too?"

Milly-Molly-Mandy was pleased.

She ran to ask Mother if she might go, and then she ran back to the little girl Jessamine and said, "Mother says thank you very much, I'd love to come!"

So the little girl Jessamine said they would fetch her about two o'clock that afternoon. And then she went back home with a basket of sweet juicy yellow gooseberries, which Father picked for her from his best gooseberry bushes.

Milly-Molly-Mandy was so excited that she wouldn't have bothered to eat any dinner at dinner-time, only Mother said she must, so she did. And then she put on her hat and coat, and Aunty lent her a nice woolly scarf, and Mother saw that her hair was tidy and that she had a clean handkerchief. And then just when she was ready she looked out of the window and saw the big motor-car drive up to the gate.

So Milly-Molly-Mandy, in a great hurry, kissed Father and Mother and Grandpa and Grandma and Uncle and Aunty good-bye (she did so wish they could have been going for a motor-ride too), and then she ran down the path to the car. And Father and Mother and Grandpa and Grandma and Uncle and Aunty all came to the door and waved, and Milly-Molly-Mandy and Mrs Green and the little girl Jessamine all waved back from the car.

And then the car went whizzing off, and the nice white cottage with the thatched roof was out of sight in a twinkling.

It was such fun to be going to the Downs! Milly-Molly-Mandy had been taken there once before by Mrs Green (with little-friend-Susan and Billy Blunt this time), and she had thought it was just the best place in the whole world for a picnic, so it was very nice to be going there again.

The little girl Jessamine and Milly-Molly-Mandy sat close together in the front seat beside Mrs Green (who drove beautifully), so that they could all see everything and talk about it together.

And they kept on seeing things all the way along. Once a partridge flew out from behind a hedge; and once a rabbit ran along in front of the car for quite a way; and once, when they were going very slowly because it was such a pretty lane with so much to see, they saw a little brown moorhen taking her baby chicks over the road ahead of them! Mrs Green quietly stopped the car so that they could watch, and the little mother moor-hen hurried across with three babies, and then two more followed her; and, after quite a long pause, another little fluffy ball went scurrying across the road in a great hurry, and they all went through a gap in the hedge out of sight.

"He nearly got left behind, didn't he?" said Mrs Green, starting the car again; and they went on, all talking about the

little moor-hen family out for a walk, and wondering where they were going.

Then presently in the road ahead they saw a bus (not the red bus that passed their village, though). And standing in the road or sitting on the grass by the side of the road were a lot of school-children (but none that Milly-Molly-Mandy knew). So Mrs Green had to slow down while they got out of the way.

As they passed they saw that the bus driver was under the bus doing something to the machinery, and the children were looking rather disappointed, and a lady who seemed to be their teacher (but not one from Milly-Molly-Mandy's school) was looking rather worried.

So Mrs Green stopped and called back, "Can we help at all?"

And the lady who seemed to be their teacher (she was their teacher) came to the side of the car, while all the children crowded round and looked on.

And the lady who was their teacher said they had all been invited to a garden-party, but the bus hired to take them kept on stopping and now it wouldn't move at all, and the lady who was their teacher didn't know quite what to do.

And then one little girl with a little pigtail said in a high little voice, "We've all got our best dresses on for the garden-party, and now we shan't be able to go-o-o!"

It did seem a pity.

Mrs Green said, "How many are there of you?"

And the lady who was their teacher said, "Sixteen, including myself."

Then Mrs Green got out and looked at her car and at all the children, and considered things. And Milly-Molly-Mandy and the little girl Jessamine sat and looked at Mrs Green and at all the children, and wondered what could be done about it. And all the children stood and looked at Mrs Green and at each other, and thought that something would be done about it, somehow.

Then Mrs Green turned to Milly-Molly-Mandy and the little girl Jessamine and said, "Shall we have our tea on the Downs or see if we can take these children to their garden-party?"

And Milly-Molly-Mandy and the little girl Jessamine of course said (both together), "Take them to the garden-party!"

So Mrs Green said, "I don't know if we can manage it, but let's see if we can all pack in!"

So everybody in great excitement tried to make themselves as small as possible, and clambered in and squeezed and shifted and sat in each other's laps and stood on

All the children crowded round and looked on

each other's toes. But still it didn't seem possible for the last two to get into the car.

Mrs Green said, "This won't do!" and she got out again and thought a bit.

And then she picked out the two smallest children and lifted them up and into the folded hood at the back of the car, and she and the lady who was their teacher tied them safely in with the belt of a coat and a stout piece of string. And there they sat above all the other children, with toes together, like babes in a cradle!

And it was Milly-Molly-Mandy and the little girl with the little pigtail who were the smallest children (and weren't they just glad!).

So everybody was in, and Mrs Green slowly drove the laden car away; and Milly-Molly-Mandy and the little girl with the little pigtail waved from their high seat to the bus driver, who stood smiling at

them and wiping his oily hands on an oily
rag.

Mrs Green drove very slowly and
carefully until they came to the big house
where the garden-party was to be. And then
everybody got out, except Milly-Molly-
Mandy and the little girl with the little
pigtail, who had to wait to be lifted down.

The lady who was giving the garden-
party was very grateful that they had been
brought, as she had prepared such a lot of
good things for them. And all the children

were so grateful too that they stood and cheered and cheered and cheered as the car drove off with just Mrs Green and the little girl Jessamine and Milly-Molly-Mandy inside.

"Wasn't that fun!" said Mrs Green.

"Won't they enjoy their garden-party!" said the little girl Jessamine.

"Wouldn't it be nice if we could all have ridden in the hood?" said Milly-Molly-Mandy.

There wasn't time now to go to the Downs for their picnic, but they found a field and spread it out there in the sunshine (and there was a cherry cake with lots of cherries in it!).

And they had such a good time. Milly-Molly-Mandy thought that field must be the best place in the world, after all, for a picnic; so it was very nice indeed that they had gone there.

Milly-Molly-Mandy
Has a Clean Frock

Once upon a time, one beautiful, fine morning, Milly-Molly-Mandy came out in a nice clean frock. (Not for any special reason; only, of course, you have to have a clean frock sometimes, and a beautiful, fine morning seems a good enough reason).

It was a Monday morning, so Mother was busy with the washing. Milly-Molly-Mandy helped her to get out the tin baths, and put up the washing-lines in the garden, and find the clothes-pegs. For with Father and Grandpa and Grandma and Uncle and Aunty and Milly-Molly-Mandy and herself to wash for, Mother always had quite a busy time on Monday mornings.

"Well, now I think that will do, thank you, Milly-Molly-Mandy," said Mother at last. "You can run off and play now".

So Milly-Molly-Mandy called Toby the dog, and they went skipping off together in the beautiful sunshine, down the road with the hedges each side, to see if little-friend-Susan or Billy Blunt were coming out to play. She had only gone as far as the big meadow gate when whom did –

14

she see but Billy Blunt (in a nice clean shirt), coming walking along up from the village. So Milly-Molly-Mandy waved hard and called out:

"Hullo, Billy! Where are you going?"

Billy Blunt just came walking on till he got near enough (so that he needn't bother to shout), and then he held up an empty jam-jar he was carrying and said:

"Tadpoles."

"Oh!" said Milly-Molly-Mandy. "Where are you going to get them? What are you going to do with them? Can I come and help you?"

Billy Blunt said:

"I want to watch them turn into frogs in our water-butt."

Milly-Molly-Mandy said:

"There's tadpoles sometimes in the pond where the cows drink."

"I know," said Billy Blunt. "That's where I'm going. Come on."

So they climbed over the top bar of the big meadow gate, and Toby the dog squeezed under the bottom bar, and they walked along a narrow little path till they came to the pond where the cows drank.

Toby the dog ran off at once to the steep part to look for water-rats. Billy Blunt and Milly-Molly-Mandy walked round to the shallow part to look for tadpoles. But the pond was getting very low, and it was very muddy and trampled there. They couldn't get close without mud coming right over their shoes.

After a while they heard Toby the dog barking excitedly, because he had found a rat-hole and wanted the owner to come out and be caught. (As if any sensible rat would!) But presently the barking turned to a splashing and yelping, so Milly-Molly-Mandy and Billy Blunt ran along the bank to see what had happened.

And – goodness me! – somehow or other Toby the dog must have slipped over the edge, for there he was, right in the pond. And he *was* in a mess! – all covered with mud and weedy stuff.

"He can't climb out there – it's too steep," said Billy Blunt. And he called, "Come on, Toby!" and tried to lead him along to where the bank was lower.

But Toby the dog just kept trying to scramble out where he had slipped in.

"He can't swim through that mud and weedy stuff, that's why," said Milly-Molly-Mandy. And she reached down to try to pull him out. But she just couldn't get him, so she reached over farther.

And then – goodness me! – somehow or

other she must have reached over too far, for next moment there was Milly-Molly-Mandy in the pond too. And she *was* in a mess! – all covered with moss and weedy stuff.

Billy Blunt said: "Well! Of all the cuckoos!" And he reached down to try to pull her out.

Milly-Molly-Mandy said: "Let's get Toby out first."

So they got Toby the dog out on to the bank. And directly he found himself there Toby the dog shook himself violently, and mud and weedy stuff flew out all round, right over Billy Blunt's clean shirt.

Billy Blunt stepped back in a hurry.

And then – goodness me! – somehow or other he must have stepped over the edge of the bank, for next moment there was Billy Blunt in the pond now (nearly on top of Milly-Molly-Mandy). And he *was* in a mess! – all covered with mud and weedy stuff.

(Milly-Molly-Mandy might have said: "Well! Of all the cuckoos!" But she was really too busy just then.)

The pond wasn't deep, and they were able to scramble out all right. But – goodness me! – you NEVER did see such a mess as Milly-Molly-Mandy and Billy Blunt and Toby the dog were in! – all covered with mud and weedy stuff.

"Oh, dear!" said Milly-Molly-Mandy. "Now what shall we do?"

"Umm," said Billy Blunt. "What will my mother say?"

"Will she be very cross?" asked Milly-Molly-Mandy. "You couldn't help it."

Billy Blunt only said: "It was a clean shirt." And he tried to squeeze the water out of it.

Milly-Molly-Mandy said: "My dress was clean too." And she tried to squeeze the water out of it.

But the more they squeezed the worse things seemed to get.

"We'd better go home," said Billy Blunt at last.

"Let's go to my home first," said Milly-Molly-Mandy. "P'raps Mother will know what to do before your mother sees you."

Billy Blunt said: "Well – I suppose I'd better see you get home all right, anyhow."

So they went across the fields and through two hedges, instead of by the road (so that nobody should see them). And they crept through the back gate into the garden of the nice white cottage with the thatched roof (where Milly-Molly-Mandy lived).

Mother was busy hanging sheets out on the line, and she didn't notice them at first.

So Milly-Molly-Mandy said: "Mother," (but not very loudly).

And Mother turned round. And she saw them standing there, Milly-Molly-Mandy, and Billy Blunt, and Toby the dog, all covered with mud and weedy stuff.

"OH!" said Mother

"We fell in the cow-pond," said Milly-Molly-Mandy in a small voice. "Toby fell in first and I tried to get him out and I fell in and Billy tried to get me out and he fell in and – we're very sorry, Mother."

And Billy Blunt nodded.

"Oh!" said Mother again.

And then she said: "Stay there!"

And she went indoors.

So Milly-Molly-Mandy and Billy Blunt and Toby the dog stayed there, wondering what Mother meant to do with them, and if she were very cross. Milly-Molly-Mandy wanted to wipe the mud off her face, but her hand was too dirty. Billy Blunt wanted to blow his nose, but his handkerchief was too wet. Toby the dog rolled in the dust to dry himself. (But it didn't make him look better.)

When Mother came out again she was carrying the tin bath she used for the washing, and after her came Aunty carrying the tin bath used for the rinsing, and they set them down on the grass. Then they went indoors and came out again, Mother with a big kettle and some soapflakes, Aunty with a big bucket and some towels. When they had put warm water in the two tin baths, Mother emptied the whole packet of soapflakes in and swished around with her hand in each till the bubbles rose up, and up, and UP.

Then Mother took Milly-Molly-Mandy, and Aunty took Billy Blunt, and they peeled the clothes off them and plopped them into the two tin baths then and there!

"Now!" said Mother. "Get busy and clean yourselves."

And she gathered up the dirty clothes into the bucket and pumped water over them at the pump.

So there were Milly-Molly-Mandy and Billy Blunt that beautiful fine morning, each in a bathful of warm bubbles nearly up to their necks, with the sheets flapping round them, and the sun shining, and the birds singing . . .

Then they got busy, swishing about in their baths, making more and yet more bubbles. They lathered their heads till they looked as if they had curly white hair and beards. They blew great coloured bubbles between their hands and watched them float off into the sky. They threw handfuls of bubbles at Toby the dog, which he tried to catch as the wind carried them away between the clothes that Mother and Aunty were pegging up on the clothes-lines.

Soon Milly-Molly-Mandy and Billy Blunt were really enjoying themselves like anything, laughing and shouting, with Toby the dog barking and the sun shining and the birds singing.

Goodness me! Those were nice baths!

And you can't think how *clean* they both felt when at last Mother made Milly-Molly-Mandy get out into a big towel and

Goodness me! Those were nice baths

hurried her indoors to put something dry on, and Billy Blunt got out into another big towel and Mother lent him some pyjamas of Father's to put on.

Then Mother washed their clothes in one of the baths and Aunty caught Toby the dog and washed him in the other. And then they threw the water out and washed the baths!

Then Milly-Molly-Mandy came out in a dressing-gown (because both her dresses were in the wash), and she and Billy Blunt, in big pyjamas, sat in the sun together, drying their hair and eating biscuits while their clothes flapped on the line and Toby the dog rolled in dust to get the cleanness off him. (He was the only one who didn't enjoy his bath.)

Mother quickly ironed up Billy Blunt's shirt and shorts and Milly-Molly-Mandy's pink-and-white striped frock. And when

they put them
on again you
would never
dream what
they had been
up to that
beautiful, fine
morning.

"Well,"
said Milly-
Molly-Mandy, "I am sorry we got so dirty,
Mother, but I *did* like that bubble-bath!"

"Yes," said Billy Blunt. "I wouldn't care
if I had to have a bubble-bath every day!"

But Mother said:

"Now listen, you two. Maybe you
couldn't help it this time. But if you come
home like that *again* you won't have
bubble-baths! I shall put you in the cow-
trough and turn the pump on you! This
has been the biggest washing-day I've had,

27

and I don't want another like it."

So then Billy Blunt said: "No, ma'am. I'm very much obliged to you, ma'am." And he thanked Aunty too.

Then he went off home in his nice clean things, sure that his mother would never dream what he had been up to.

But when Mrs Blunt saw him come in (rather late for dinner, but looking so clean and tidy) she guessed he had been up to *something*. And when she saw his muddy shoes, and found he hadn't caught any tadpoles and didn't know what he had done with his jam-jar, she pretty well guessed everything.

But Mrs Blunt never dreamed what grand bubble-baths Billy Blunt and Milly-Molly-Mandy had had, out in the garden of the nice white cottage with the thatched roof that beautiful fine morning!

Milly-Molly-Mandy
Writes Letters

Once upon a time Milly-Molly-Mandy heard the postman's knock, bang-BANG! on the front door; so she ran hop-skip down the passage to look in the letter-box, because she always sort of hoped there might be a letter for her!

But there wasn't.

"I do wish the postman would bring me a letter sometimes," said Milly-Molly-Mandy,

coming slowly back into the kitchen. "He never does. There's only a business-looking letter for Father and an advertisement for Uncle."

And then Milly-Molly-Mandy noticed that the business-looking letter was from Holland (where Father got his flower bulbs) and had a Dutch stamp on it, so that was more interesting. Milly-Molly-Mandy was collecting foreign stamps. She had collected one Irish one already, and it was stuck in Billy Blunt's new stamp album. (Billy Blunt had just started collecting stamps, so Milly-Molly-Mandy was collecting for him.)

"If you want the postman to bring you letters you'll have to write them to other people first," said Mother, putting the letters upon the mantelshelf till

Father and Uncle should come in.

"But I haven't got any stamps," said Milly-Molly-Mandy.

"I'll give you one when you want it," said Grandma, pulling the kettle forward on the stove.

"But I don't know who to write to," said Milly-Molly-Mandy.

"You'll have to think round a little," said Aunty, clearing her sewing off the table.

"There's only Billy Blunt and little-friend-Susan, and it would be silly to write to them when I see them every day," said Milly-Molly-Mandy.

"We must just think," said Mother, spreading the cloth on the table for tea. "There are sure to be lots of people who would like to have letters by post, as well as you."

Milly-Molly-Mandy hadn't thought of that. "Do you suppose they'd run like anything to the letter-box because they thought there might be a letter from me?" she said. "What fun! I've got the fancy notepaper that Aunty gave me at Christmas – they'll like that, won't they? Who can I write to?"

And then she helped to lay the table, and made a piece of toast at the fire for Grandma; and presently Father and Uncle and Grandpa came in to tea, and Milly-Molly-Mandy was given the Dutch stamp off Father's letter. She put it in her pencil-box, ready for Billy Blunt in the morning.

And then she had an idea. "If I could write to someone not in England they'd stick foreign stamps on their letters when they wrote back, wouldn't they?"

And then Aunty had an idea. "Why, there are my little nieces in America!" she said. (For Aunty had a brother who went to America when he was quite young, and now he had three little children, whom none of them had seen or knew hardly anything about, for "Tom", as Aunty called him, wasn't a very good letter writer, and only wrote to her sometimes at Christmas.)

"Ooh, yes!" said Milly-Molly-Mandy, "and I don't believe Billy has an American stamp yet. What are their names, Aunty? I forget."

"Sally and Lallie," said Aunty, "and the boy is Tom, after my brother, but they call him Buddy. They would like to have a letter from their cousin in England, I'm sure."

So Milly-Molly-Mandy looked out the box of fancy notepaper that Aunty had given her, and kept it by her side while she did her home-lessons after tea. And then, when she had done them all, she wrote quite a long letter to her cousin Sallie (at least it looked quite a long letter, because the pink notepaper was rather small), telling about her school, and her friends, and Billy Blunt's collection, and about Toby the dog, and Topsy the cat, and what Father and Mother and Grandpa and Grandma and Uncle and Aunty were all doing at that moment in the kitchen, and outside in the barn; so that Sallie should get to know them all. And then there was just room to send her love to Lallie and Buddy, and to sign her name.

It was quite a nice letter.

Milly-Molly-Mandy showed it to Mother and Aunty, and then (just to make it more interesting) she put in a piece of coloured silver paper and two primroses (the first she had found that year), and stuck down the flap of the pink envelope.

The next morning she posted her letter in the red pillar-box on the way to school (little-friend-Susan was quite interested when she showed her the address); and then she tried to forget all about it, because she knew it would take a long while to get

there and a
longer while
still for an answering letter to come back.

After morning school she gave the Dutch stamp to Billy Blunt for his collection. He said he had got one, as they were quite common, but that it might come in useful for exchanging with some other fellow. And after school that very afternoon he told her he had exchanged it for a German stamp; so it was very useful.

"Have you got an American stamp?" asked Milly-Molly-Mandy.

"No," said Billy Blunt. "What I want to get hold of is a Czechoslovakian one. Ted Smale's just got one. His uncle gave it to him."

Milly-Molly-Mandy didn't think she could ever collect such a stamp as that for Billy Blunt, but she was glad he hadn't got an American one yet.

All that week and the next Milly-Molly-

Mandy rushed to the letter-box every time she heard the postman, although she knew there wouldn't be an answer for about three weeks, anyhow. But the postman's knock, bang-BANG! sounded so exciting she always forgot to remember in time.

A whole month went by, and Milly-Molly-Mandy began almost to stop expecting a letter at all, or at least one from abroad.

And then one day she came home after school a bit later than usual, because she and little-friend-Susan had been picking wind-flowers and primroses under a hedge, very excited to think spring had really come. But when she did get in what DO you think she found waiting for her, on her plate at the table?

Why, *three* letters, just come by post! One from Sallie, one from Lallie, and one from Buddy!

They sat and wrote letters together

They were so pleased at having a letter from England that they had all written back, hoping she would write again. And they sent some snapshots of themselves, and Buddy enclosed a Japanese stamp for Billy Blunt's collection.

The next Saturday Billy Blunt came to tea with Milly-Molly-Mandy and she gave him the four stamps, three American and one Japanese. And, though he said they were not really valuable ones, he was pleased as anything to have them!

And when the table was cleared they sat and wrote letters together – Milly-Molly-Mandy to Sallie and Lallie, and Billy Blunt to Buddy (to thank him for the stamp), with a little P.S. from Milly-Molly-Mandy (to thank him for his letter).

Milly-Molly-Mandy does like letter-writing because now she has got three more friends!

Milly-Molly-Mandy Has a New Dress

Once upon a time Milly-Molly-Mandy was playing hide-and-seek with Toby the dog.

First Milly-Molly-Mandy threw a stone as far as she could, and then while Toby the dog was fetching it Milly-Molly-Mandy ran the other way and hid in among the gooseberry and currant bushes or behind the wall. And then Toby the dog came to look for her. He was so clever he always found her almost at once – even when she hid in the stable where Twinkletoes the pony lived (only he was out in the meadow

eating grass now).

She shut the lower half of the stable door and kept quite quiet, but Toby the dog barked and scratched outside, and wouldn't go away till Milly-Molly-Mandy pushed open the door and came out.

Then Toby the dog was so pleased to see her, and so pleased with himself for finding her, that he jumped up and down on his hind legs, pawing and scratching at her skirt.

And suddenly – rrrrrip! – there was a great big tear all the way down the front of Milly-Molly-Mandy's pink-and-white striped cotton frock.

"Oh dear, oh dear!" said Milly-Molly-

Mandy. "Oh, Toby, just see what you've done now!"

Then Toby the dog stopped jumping up and down, and he looked very sorry and ashamed of himself. So Milly-Molly-Mandy said, "All right, then! Poor Toby! You didn't mean to do it. But whatever will Mother say? I'll have to go and show her."

So Milly-Molly-Mandy, looking very solemn and holding her dress together with both hands, walked back through the barnyard where the cows were milked (only they, too, were out in the meadow eating grass now).

Uncle was throwing big buckets of water over the floor of the cowshed, to wash it.

"Now what have you been up to?" he asked, as Milly-Molly-Mandy, looking very solemn and holding her dress together with both hands, passed by.

"I tore my dress playing with Toby, and

I'm going to show Mother," said Milly-Molly-Mandy.

"Well, well," said Uncle, sending another big bucketful of water swashing along over the brick floor. "Now you'll catch it. Tell Mother to send you out to me if she wants you to get a good spanking. I'll give you a proper one!"

"Mother won't let you spank me!" said Milly-Molly-Mandy (she knew Uncle was only joking). "But she won't like having to mend such a great big tear, I expect. She mended this dress only a little while ago, and now it's got to be done all over again. Come on, Toby."

So they went through the gate into the kitchen garden (where Father grew the vegetables) and in by the back door of the nice white cottage with the thatched roof where Father and Mother and Grandpa and Grandma and Uncle and Aunty and, of course, Milly-Molly-Mandy all lived together.

"Now what's the matter with little Millicent Margaret Amanda?" said Grandma, who was shelling peas for dinner, as Milly-Molly-Mandy came in, looking very solemn and holding her dress together with both hands.

"I'm looking for Mother," said Milly-Molly-Mandy.

"She's in the larder," said Aunty, who was patching sheets with her machine at the kitchen table. "What have you been up to?"

But Milly-Molly-Mandy went over to the door of the larder, where Mother was washing the shelves.

"Mother," said Milly-Molly-Mandy, looking very solemn and holding her dress together with both hands, "I'm dreadfully sorry, but I was playing hide-and-seek with Toby, and we tore my dress. Badly."

"Dear, dear, now!" said Grandma.

"Whatever next!" said Aunty.

"Let me have a look," said Mother. She put down her wash-cloth and came out into the kitchen.

Milly-Molly-Mandy took her hands away and showed her frock, with the great big tear all down the front of it.

Mother looked at it. And then she said:

"Well, Milly-Molly-Mandy! That just about finishes that frock! But I was afraid it couldn't last much longer when I mended it before."

And Grandma said, "She had really outgrown it."

And Aunty said, "It was very faded."

And Mother said, "You will have to have a new one."

Milly-Molly-Mandy was pleased to think that was all they said about it. (So was Toby the dog!)

Mother said, "You can go out in the garden and tear it all you like now, Milly-Molly-Mandy. But don't you go tearing anything else!"

So Milly-Molly-Mandy and Toby the dog had a fine time tearing her old dress to ribbons, so that she looked as if she had been dancing in a furze bush, Grandpa said. And then Mother sent her upstairs to change into her better frock (which was pink-and-white striped, too).

During dinner Mother said, "I'm going to take Milly-Molly-Mandy down to the village this afternoon, to buy her some stuff for a new dress."

Father said, "I suppose that means you

want some more money." And he took some out of his trousers' pocket and handed it over to Mother.

Grandma said, "What about getting her something that isn't pink-and-white striped, just for a change?"

Grandpa said, "Let's have flowers instead of stripes this time."

Aunty said, "Something with daisies on would look nice."

Uncle said, "Oh, let's go gay while we are about it, and have magenta roses and yellow sunflowers – eh, Milly-Molly-Mandy?"

But Milly-Molly-Mandy said, "I don't 'spect Miss Muggins keeps that sort of stuff in her shop, so then I can't have it!"

After dinner Milly-Molly-Mandy helped Mother to wash up the plates and things, and then Mother changed her dress, and they put on their hats, and Mother took her handbag, and they went

Milly-Molly-Mandy showed her dress with the tear all down the front

together down the road with the hedges each side towards the village.

They passed the Moggses' cottage, where little-friend-Susan lived. Little-friend-Susan was helping her baby sister to make mud pies on the step.

"Hullo, Susan," said Milly-Molly-Mandy. "We're going to buy me some different new dress stuff at Miss Muggins's shop, because I tore my other one!"

"Are you? How nice! What colour are you going to have this time?" asked little-friend-Susan.

"We don't know yet, but it will be something quite different," said Milly-Molly-Mandy.

They passed the Forge, where Mr Rudge the Blacksmith and his new boy were making a big fire over an iron hoop which, when it was red-hot, they were going to fit round a broken cart-wheel to mend it.

Milly-Molly-Mandy wanted to stay and watch, but Mother said she hadn't time.

So Milly-Molly-Mandy just called out to Mr Rudge, "We're going to buy some different coloured dress stuff, because I tore my other one!"

And Mr Rudge stopped to wipe his hot face on his torn shirt sleeve, and said, "Well, if they'd buy us different-coloured shirts every time we tear ours, you'd see us going about like a couple of rainbows! Eh, Reginald?"

And the new boy grinned as he piled more brushwood on the fire. (He'd got a tear in his shirt too.)

They passed Mr Blunt's corn-shop, where Billy Blunt was polishing up his new second-hand bicycle, which his father had just given him, on the pavement outside.

Milly-Molly-Mandy and Mother stopped a minute to admire its shininess

(which was almost like new). And then Milly-Molly-Mandy said, "We're going to buy me some different-coloured dress stuff, because I tore my other!"

But Billy Blunt wasn't very interested (he was just testing his front brake).

Then they came to Miss Muggins's shop.

And just as they got up to the door so did two other people, coming from the other way. One was an old lady in a black cloak and bonnet, and one was a little girl in a faded flowered dress, with a ribbon round her hair. Mother pushed open the shop door for the old lady and set the little bell jangling above, and they all went in together, so that the shop seemed quite full of people, with Miss Muggins behind the counter too.

Miss Muggins didn't know quite whom to serve first. She looked towards the old lady, and the old lady looked towards Mother, and Mother said, "No, you first."

So then the old lady said, "I would like to see something for a dress for a little girl, if you please – something light and summery."

And Mother said, "That is exactly what I am wanting, too."

So then Miss Muggins brought out the different stuffs from her shelves for both her customers to choose from together.

Milly-Molly-Mandy looked at the little girl. She thought she had seen her before. Surely it was the new little girl who had lately come to Milly-Molly-Mandy's school. Only she was in the "baby class", so they hadn't talked together yet.

The little girl looked at Milly-Molly-Mandy. And presently she pulled at the old lady's arm and whispered something, whereupon the old lady turned and smiled at Milly-Molly-Mandy, so Milly-Molly-Mandy smiled back.

Milly-Molly-Mandy whispered up at Mother (looking at the little girl). "She comes to our school!"

So then Mother smiled at the little girl. And the old lady and Mother began to talk together as they looked at Miss Muggins's stuffs. And Milly-Molly-Mandy and the little girl began to talk too, as they waited.

Milly-Molly-Mandy found out that the little girl

was called Bunchy, and the old lady was her grandmother, and they lived together in a little cottage quite a long way from the school and the crossroads, in the other direction from Milly-Molly-Mandy's.

Bunchy hadn't come to school before because she couldn't walk so far. But now she was bigger, and Granny walked with her half the way and she ran the rest by herself.

She liked coming to school, but she had never played with other little girls and boys before, and it all felt very strange and rather frightening. So then Milly-Molly-Mandy said they should look out for each other at school next Monday, and play together during play-time. And she told her about little-friend-Susan, and Billy Blunt, and Miss Muggins's Jilly, and other friends at school.

Then Mother said to Miss Muggins, "And this is all you have in the way of printed cottons? Well, now, I wonder, Milly-Molly-Mandy."

And Bunchy's grandmother said, "Look here, Bunchy, my dear."

So they both went up to the counter.

There was a light blue silky stuff which Mother and Bunchy's grandmother said was "not serviceable". And a stuff with scarlet poppies and cornflowers all over it which they said was "not suitable". And there was a green chintz stuff which they said was too thick. And a yellow muslin which they said was too thin.

And there was a stuff with little bunches of daisies and forget-me-nots on it. And a big roll of pink-and-white striped cotton. And there was nothing more (except flannelette or bolton-sheeting and that sort of thing, which wouldn't do at all).

Milly-Molly-Mandy thought the one with daisies and forget-me-nots was much the prettiest.

So did Bunchy. Milly-Molly-Mandy thought a dress of that would be a very nice change.

But Miss Muggins said, "I'm afraid I have only this 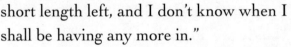 short length left, and I don't know when I shall be having any more in."

So Mother and Bunchy's grandmother spread it out, and there was really only just enough to make one little frock. Bunchy's grandmother turned to look at the pink-and-white striped stuff.

Bunchy said, "That's Milly-Molly-Mandy's stuff, isn't it? It's just like the dress she has on."

Milly-Molly-Mandy said, "Do you always have flowers on your dresses?"

"Yes," said Bunchy, "because of my name, you know. I'm Violet Rosemary May, but Granny calls me Bunchy for short."

Milly-Molly-Mandy said to Mother, "She ought to have that stuff with the bunches of flowers on, oughtn't she? The striped one wouldn't really suit her so well as me, would it?"

Mother said, "Well, Milly-Molly-Mandy, we do know this striped stuff suits you all right, and it washes and wears well. I'm afraid that blue silky stuff doesn't look as if it would wash, and the yellow muslin wouldn't wear. So perhaps you'd better have the same again. I'll take two yards of this striped, please, Miss Muggins."

Milly-Molly-Mandy looked once more at the flowery stuff, and she said, "It is pretty, isn't it! But if Bunchy comes to school I can see it on her, can't I?"

Bunchy's grandmother said, "It would be very nice if you could come and see it on Bunchy at home too! If Mother would bring you to tea one Saturday, if you don't mind rather a walk, you could play in the garden with Bunchy, and I'm sure we should both be very pleased indeed, shouldn't we, Bunchy?"

Bunchy said, "Yes! We should!"

Mother said, "Thank you very much. We should like to come" – though she had not much time for going out to tea as a rule, but she was sure Aunty would get tea for them all at home for once.

So it was settled for them to go next Saturday, and the little girl called Bunchy was very pleased indeed about it, and so was Milly-Molly-Mandy.

Then Miss Muggins handed over the counter the two parcels, and Milly-Molly-Mandy and Bunchy each carried her own dress stuff home.

And when Milly-Molly-Mandy opened her parcel to show Father and Grandpa and Grandma and Uncle and Aunty what had been bought for her new dress after all, there was a beautiful shiny red ribbon there too, which Mother had bought to tie round Milly-Molly-Mandy's hair when she wore the new dress. So that would make quite a nice change, anyhow.

And as little-
friend-Susan said,
if Milly-Molly-
Mandy didn't wear
her pink-and white
stripes people
might not know her
at once.

And that would be a pity!

Milly-Molly-Mandy Gets Locked In

Once upon a time Milly-Molly-Mandy got locked in her little bedroom (which had been the little storeroom up under the thatched roof).

No, she hadn't been naughty or anything like that, and nobody locked her in. But the latch on the door had gone just a bit wrong, somehow, so that once or twice Milly-Molly-Mandy had had to turn the handle several times before she could open it; so Mother said perhaps she had better not close it quite, till Father found time to mend it.

But one Saturday morning, when Milly-Molly-Mandy had helped Mother with the breakfast things and Aunty with the beds, she went up to her own little room to make the bed there, and Topsy the cat ran up with her.

Now Topsy the cat just loved Milly-Molly-Mandy to make her bed on Saturdays mornings.

She would jump into the middle of the mattress and crouch down; and then Milly-Molly-Mandy would pretend not to know Topsy the cat was there at all. And she would thump the pillows and roll Topsy the cat about with them, and whisk the sheets and blankets over and pretend to try to smooth out the lump that was Topsy the cat underneath; and Topsy the cat would come crawling out, looking very untidy, and make a dive under the next blanket. (And it took quite a long while to make that bed sometimes!)

Well, Milly-Molly-Mandy had got the bed made at last, and then she was so out of breath she backed up against the door to rest a bit, while Topsy the cat sat in the middle of the coverlet to tidy herself up.

And it wasn't until Milly-Molly-Mandy had tidied her own hair and had wrapped her duster round Topsy the cat (so as to carry them both downstairs together) that she found she couldn't open the door, which had shut with a bang when she leaned against it!

"Well!" said Milly-Molly-Mandy to Topsy the cat, "now what are we going to do?" She put Topsy the cat down and tried the door again.

But she couldn't open it.

Then she called "Mother!" But Mother

was downstairs in the kitchen, getting bowls and baking-tins ready for making cakes (as it was Saturday morning).

Then Milly-Molly-Mandy called "Aunty!" But Aunty was in the parlour, giving it an extra good dusting (as it wouldn't get much next day, being Sunday).

Then Milly-Molly-Mandy called "Grandma!" But Grandma was round by the back door, sprinkling crumbs for the birds (as it was just their busy time with all the hungry baby-birds hatching out).

"Well!" said Milly-Molly-Mandy to Topsy the cat, "this *is* a waste of a nice fine Saturday!"

She went to the little low window, but the only person she could see was Uncle, looking like a little speck at the farther end of the meadow, doing something to his chicken-houses. Father, she knew, had gone to the next village to give someone advice about a garden; and Grandpa had gone to market.

"Well!" said Milly-Molly-Mandy to Topsy the cat, "if I'd only got legs like a grasshopper I could just jump down – but I'd rather have my own legs, anyhow!"

Then she thought if she had a long enough piece of string she could touch the ground that way, and if she dangled it someone might see from the downstairs windows.

So she took the cord from her dressing-gown, and she tied to it a piece of string from her coat-pocket. And a piece of mauve ribbon which Aunty had given her. And the belt from her frock. And her two boot-laces (Topsy the cat got quite interested). And then she tied her little yellow basket on the end, and dangled and swung it out of the window backward and forward in front of the scullery window below.

But nobody came, and at last Milly-Molly-Mandy got tired of this and tied the end of the line on to the window-catch, and drew her head in again.

"Well!" said Milly-Molly-Mandy to Topsy the cat. "It's a good thing I've got such a nice little bedroom to be shut up in, anyhow!" Topsy the cat just turned herself round and round on the bed and settled down for a sleep.

Then Milly-Molly-Mandy suddenly remembered her crochet work, carefully wrapped up in a handkerchief on her little green chest of drawers. It was to be a bonnet for Baby Moggs (little-friend-Susan's new little sister and own nearly-sister). It was of pale pink wool, and she was making it rather big because Mother thought Baby Moggs might grow a bit before the bonnet was finished. (Milly-Molly-Mandy did hope Baby Moggs wouldn't grow too fast.)

So Milly-Molly-Mandy sat in the middle of the floor and began crocheting.

Crocheting is quite hard work when you've done only three and a half rows in all your life before, but Milly-Molly-Mandy crocheted and crocheted until she reached the end of the row; and then she turned round and crocheted and crocheted all the way back. So that was a row and a half.

Then she heard the window-catch on which her line was tied give a little click, and she jumped up and looked out to see if someone were touching her line. But nobody was about, though she called.

But it looked as if there was something in the little yellow basket, so Milly-Molly-

Mandy pulled it up in a hurry. And what do you think? In the little yellow basket was a little paperful of that nice crunchy sugar which comes inside the big lumps of peel you put in cakes. (Mother had thought the basket and line was just a game of Milly-Molly-Mandy's, and she popped the sugar in for a surprise.)

"How nice!" thought Milly-Molly-Mandy, and she dropped the little yellow basket outside again (hoping something else would be put in it) and went back to her crochet-work. And she crocheted and crunched, and crunched and crocheted, until she had done four whole rows and eaten up all the paperful of sugar.

Then, after all this time, Milly-Molly-Mandy heard Mother's voice calling outside:

"Milly-Molly-Mandy!"

And when Milly-Molly-Mandy jumped

up and looked out, Mother (who had come to see if there was enough rhubarb up yet to make a tart) said, "What are you doing, dear? You ought to be outdoors!"

So Milly-Molly-Mandy was able to tell Mother all about it; and then Mother came running up to Milly-Molly-Mandy's bedroom door.

But Mother couldn't open it, though she tried hard – and neither could Aunty.

So Mother kissed Milly-Molly-Mandy through the crack, and said she must just wait till Father came home and then he would get her out. And Milly-Molly-Mandy kissed Mother back through the crack, and sat down to her crochet-work again.

Presently the line outside the window clicked at the catch again, and Milly-Molly-Mandy looked out just in time to see Mother whisking out of sight round the corner of the cottage, and there was a big red apple in the little yellow basket! So Milly-Molly-Mandy pulled it up again, and then went back and did her crocheting between big bites at the big red apple.

And she crocheted and she crocheted and she crocheted.

Just before dinner-time Father came back, and Mother took him straight up to Milly-Molly-Mandy's bedroom door, and they tinkered about with the lock for a while, rattling and clicking and tapping.

And Milly-Molly-Mandy went on crocheting.

Then Father said through the crack, "I'll have to break the lock, Milly-Molly-Mandy, so you mustn't mind a noise!"

Milly-Molly-Mandy put her crochet-work down, and said, "No, Father!" (It was rather exciting!)

Then Father fetched a great big hammer,

and he gave some great big bangs on the lock, and the door came bursting open in a great hurry, and Father and Mother came in. (They had to stoop their heads in Milly-Molly-Mandy's room, because it was so little and sloping.)

Milly-Molly-Mandy was so pleased to see them.

She held up her crochet-work and said, "Look! I've crocheted nine whole rows and I haven't dropped one single stitch! Don't you think it's enough now, before you start doing it different to make it fit at the back?"

And Mother said, "That's fine, Milly-Molly-Mandy! I'll look at it directly after dinner and see, but you'd better come downstairs now."

So Milly-Molly-Mandy came downstairs, and they all had dinner and talked about locks and about getting new ones.

And then Mother looked at Milly-Molly-Mandy's crochet-work. And it only wanted just a little more doing to it (most of which Mother showed Milly-Molly-Mandy how to do, but some she had to do herself); and quite soon the bonnet was finished, and Milly-Molly-Mandy took it round to the Moggses' cottage in tissue paper.

Mrs Moggs and little-friend-Susan looked at it most admiringly, and then Mrs Moggs put it on Baby Moggs's head and tied it under her soft little chin.

And it just fitted Baby Moggs perfectly!

(But, you know, as Milly-Molly-Mandy crocheted very tightly indeed – being her first try – it was a good thing she had planned to leave enough room for Baby Moggs to grow, and a very good thing she got locked in and finished it before

It just fitted Baby Moggs perfectly!

Baby Moggs had any time to grow, for the bonnet was only just big enough.

(But you can't *think* what a darling Baby Moggs looked in it!)

Milly-Molly-Mandy
Gives a Party

Once upon a time Milly-Molly-Mandy
had a plan. And when she had thought
over the plan for a while she went to look
in her money-box. And in the money-
box were four pennies and a ha'penny,
which Milly-Molly-Mandy did not think
would be enough for her plan. So Milly-
Molly-Mandy went off to talk it over with
little-friend-Susan down the road.

"Susan," said Milly-Molly-Mandy,
"I've got a plan (only it's a great secret). I
want to give a party in our barn to Farver
and Muvver and Grandpa and Grandma

and Uncle and Aunty. And I want to buy refreshments. And you and I will be waitresses. And if there's anything over we can eat it up afterwards."

Little-friend-Susan thought it a very good plan indeed.

"Will we wear caps?" she asked.

"Yes," said Milly-Molly-Mandy, "and aprons. Only I haven't got enough money for the refreshments, so I don't think there'll be any over. We must think."

So Milly-Molly-Mandy and little-friend-Susan sat down and thought hard.

"We must work and earn some," said Milly-Molly-Mandy.

"But how?" said little-friend-Susan.

"We might sell something," said Milly-Molly-Mandy.

"But what?" said little-friend-Susan. So they had to think some more.

Presently Milly-Molly-Mandy said,

"I've got pansies and marigolds in my garden."

And little-friend-Susan said, "I've got nasturtiums in mine."

"We could run errands for people," said Milly-Molly-Mandy.

"And clean brass," said little-friend-Susan.

That was a lovely idea, so Milly-Molly-Mandy fetched a pencil and paper and wrote out very carefully:

Millicent Margaret Amanda & Susan & Co. have bunches of flowers for sale and clean brass very cheap (we do not spill the polish) and run errands very cheap.

"What's 'and Co.'?" said little-friend-Susan.

"It's just business," said Milly-Molly-Mandy, "but perhaps we might ask Billy Blunt to be it. And he could be a waiter."

Then they hung the notice on the front

gate, and waited just the other side of the hedge.

Several people passed, but nobody seemed to want anything. Then at last a motor-car came along with a lady and gentleman in it; and when they saw the nice white cottage with the thatched roof they stopped at the gate to ask if they could get some cream there.

Milly-Molly-Mandy said, "I'll go and ask Muvver," and took the little pot they held out. And when she came back with it full of cream the lady and gentleman had read the notice and were asking little-friend-Susan questions. As the lady paid for the cream she said they must certainly have some flowers. So they each bought a bunch. And then the gentleman said the round brass thing in front of his car needed cleaning very badly – could the firm do it straight away?

So Milly-Molly-Mandy said, "Yes, sir," and raced back to the cottage to give Mother the cream-money and to borrow the brass-polishing box. And then she cleaned the round brass thing in front of the car with one piece of cloth and little-friend-Susan rubbed it bright with another piece of cloth, and the lady and gentleman looked on and seemed very satisfied.

Then the gentleman asked, "How much?" and paid them two pence for the flowers and a penny for the polishing. Milly-Molly-Mandy wanted to do some more polishing for the money, but the gentleman said they couldn't stop. And then they said goodbye and went off, and the lady turned and waved, and Milly-Molly-Mandy and little-friend-Susan waved back until they were gone.

Milly-Molly-Mandy and little-friend-Susan felt very happy and pleased.

And now they had sevenpence-ha'penny for the refreshments. Father and Mother and Grandpa and Grandma and Uncle and Aunty and Mrs Moggs, little-friend-Susan's mother, made seven.

Then who should look over the hedge but Mr Jakes, the Postman, on his way home from collecting letters from the letter-boxes. He had seen the notice on the gate.

"What's this? You trying to make a fortune?" said the Postman.

"Yes," said Milly-Molly-Mandy, "we've earned three pence!"

"My! And what do you plan to do with it?" said the Postman.

"We've got a secret!" said Milly-Molly-Mandy, with a little skip.

"Ah!" said the Postman, "I guess it's a nice one, too!"

Milly-Molly-Mandy looked at little-friend-Susan, and then she looked at the

Postman. He was a nice Postman. "You won't tell if we tell you?" she asked.

"Try me!" said the Postman promptly. So Milly-Molly-Mandy told him they were planning to give a party to Father and Mother and Grandpa and Grandma and Uncle and Aunty and Mrs Moggs.

"They're in luck, they are!" said the Postman. "Nobody asks me to parties."

Milly-Molly-Mandy looked at little-friend-Susan again, and then she looked at the Postman. He was a very nice Postman. Then she said, "Supposing you were invited, would you come?"

"You try me!" said the Postman promptly again. And then he hitched up his letter-bag and went on.

"Farver and Muvver and Grandpa and Grandma and Uncle and Aunty and Mrs Moggs and the Postman. We've got to earn some more," said Milly-Molly-Mandy. "Let's go down to the village and ask Billy Blunt to be 'and Co.', and p'r'aps he'll have an idea."

Billy Blunt was in the road outside the corn-shop, mending the handles of his box on wheels. He had made it nearly all himself, and it was a very nice one, painted green like the water-butt and the lawn roller. He thought "and Co." was rather a funny name, but he said he would be it all right, and offered to make them a box with a slit in it, where they could keep their earnings. And he put in four farthings out of his collection. (Billy Blunt was collecting farthings – he had nineteen in an empty bird seed bag.)

So now they had eightpence-ha'penny for the refreshments.

On Monday morning, on their way home to dinner, Milly-Molly-Mandy and little-friend-Susan passed Mrs Jakes, the Postman's wife, at her door, getting a breath of fresh air before dishing up her dinner.

And Mrs Jakes said, "Good morning! How's the firm of Millicent Margaret Amanda, Susan and Co. getting on?"

Milly-Molly-Mandy said, "Very well, thank you!"

"My husband's told me about your brass-cleaning," said Mrs Jakes. "I've got a whole mantel-shelf full that wants doing!"

Milly-Molly-Mandy and little-friend-Susan were very pleased, and arranged to come in directly school was over in the afternoon and clean it.

And they cleaned a mug and three candlesticks and two lamps – one big and one little – and a tray and a warming-pan, and they didn't spill or waste any of the polish. Mrs Jakes seemed very satisfied, and gave them each a penny and a piece of cake.

So now they had tenpence-ha'penny for refreshments.

But when they got outside Milly-Molly-

Mandy said, "Farver and Muvver and Grandpa and Grandma and Uncle and Aunty and Mrs Moggs and the Postman and Mrs Postman – I wonder if we've earned enough, Susan!"

As they turned home they passed the forge, and of course they had to stop a moment at the doorway, as usual, to watch the fire roaring, and Mr Rudge the Blacksmith banging with his hammer on the anvil.

Little-friend-Susan was just a bit nervous of the Blacksmith – he was so big, and his face was so dirty it made his teeth look very white and his eyes very twinkly when he smiled at them. But Milly-Molly-Mandy knew he was nice and clean under the dirt, which he couldn't help while he worked. So she smiled back.

And the Blacksmith said, "Hullo!"

And Milly-Molly-Mandy said, "Hullo!"

Then the Blacksmith beckoned with his finger and said, "Come here!"

Milly-Molly-Mandy gave a little jump, and little-friend-Susan pulled at her hand, but Milly-Molly-Mandy knew he was really just a nice man under the dirt, so she went up to him.

And the Blacksmith said, "Look what I've got here!" And he showed them a tiny little horseshoe, just like a proper one, only smaller, which he had made for them to keep. Milly-Molly-Mandy and little-friend-Susan were pleased!

Milly-Molly-Mandy thanked him very much. And then she looked at the Blacksmith and said, "If you were invited to a party, would you come?"

And the Blacksmith looked at Milly-Molly-Mandy with twinkly eyes and said he'd come quite fast – so long as it wasn't before five o'clock on Saturday, when he was playing cricket with his team in the meadow.

When they got outside again Milly-Molly-Mandy said, "Farver and Muvver and Grandpa and Grandma and Uncle and Aunty and Mrs Moggs and the Postman and Mrs Postman and the Blacksmith. We'll ask them for half-past five, and we ought to earn some more money, Susan!"

Just then they met Billy Blunt coming along, pulling his box on wheels with a bundle in it.

And Billy Blunt grinned and said, "I'm fetching Mrs Bloss's washing, for the firm!" Milly-Molly-Mandy and little-friend-Susan were pleased!

When Saturday morning came all the invitations had been given out, and the firm of Millicent Margaret Amanda, Susan and Co. was very busy putting things tidy in the barn, and covering up things which couldn't be moved with lots of green branches which Grandpa was trimming from the hedges.

And when half-past five came Milly-Molly-Mandy and little-friend-Susan, with clean hands and paper caps and aprons, waited by the barn door to welcome the guests. And each gentleman received a marigold buttonhole, and each lady a pansy.

Everybody arrived in good time, except the Blacksmith, who was just a bit late – he looked so clean and pink in his white cricket flannels, Milly-Molly-Mandy hardly knew him – and Billy Blunt. But Billy Blunt came lugging a gramophone and two records which he had borrowed from a bigger boy at school. (He never told, but he had given the boy all the rest of his collection of farthings – fifteen of them, which makes three-pence-three-farthings – in exchange.)

Then Billy Blunt, who didn't want to dance, looked after the gramophone, while

Father and Mother and Grandpa and Grandma and Uncle and Aunty and Mrs Moggs and the Postman and Mrs Postman and the Blacksmith and Milly-Molly-Mandy and little-friend-Susan danced together in the old barn till the dust flew. And Milly-Molly-Mandy danced a lot with the Blacksmith as well as with everybody else, and so did little-friend-Susan.

They did enjoy themselves!

And then there were refreshments – raspberry drops and aniseed balls on saucers trimmed with little flowers; and late blackberries on leaf plates; and sherbet drinks, which Billy Blunt prepared while Milly-Molly-Mandy and little-friend-Susan stood by to tell people just the very moment to drink, when it was fizzing properly. (It was exciting!) And a jelly which Milly-Molly-Mandy and little-friend-Susan had made themselves from a

And then there were refreshments!

packet, only it had to be eaten rather like soup, as it wouldn't stand up properly.

But Father and Mother and Grandpa and Grandma and Uncle and Aunty and Mrs Moggs and the Postman and Mrs Postman and the Blacksmith all said they had never enjoyed a jelly so much. And the Blacksmith, in a big voice, proposed a vote of thanks to the firm for the delightful party and refreshments, and everybody else said "Hear! Hear!" and clapped. And Milly-Molly-Mandy and little-friend-Susan joined in the clapping too, which wasn't quite proper, but they were so happy they couldn't help it!

And then all the guests went home.

And when the firm came to clear up the refreshments they found there was only one aniseed ball left. But placed among the empty saucers and glasses on the bench were a small basket of pears and a bag of mixed sweets with a ticket "For the Waiter and Waitresses" on it!

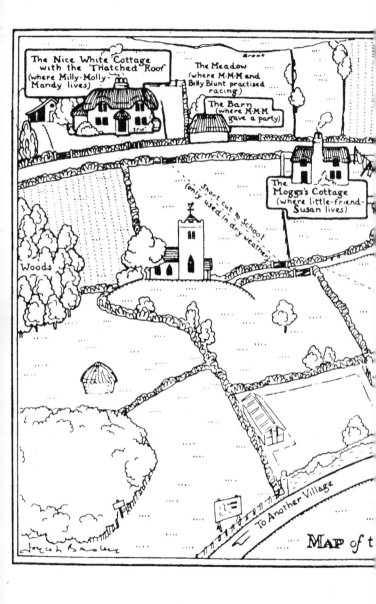